I0608539

THE ENEMY
WITHIN

Michelle Rhnea Yisrael

Published by I AM Media Books

ISBN: 978-1-951667-04-7
Published by I AM Media Books, Michigan, USA
Media to Awaken the World!

www.iammediabooks.com

Dedicated to the survivors; and all my sisters who are dying inside and fighting to stay alive.

A Woman's Prayer of Hope

Now I lay me down to sleep
My faith in Yah I hope to keep
Filled with hurt instilled down deep
Filled with all the victories I reap
A careful blend of life's many spices
Walking the straight and narrow avoiding
Satan's devices
Turning away from all evil entices
Obedience is better than any sacrifices
If I should die before I wake
I pray for forgiveness of any mistake
Seeking New Jerusalem and escaping the
lake Save me Father for your name's sake
Guide my husband, as he is my head
Leading with benevolence as your word said
Now I lay me down to rest
I pray that I have passed my test
Bless my children from any heartache
Bless them Jesus so they too may partake
Now I lay me down to sleep
Comfort me Yahuah so no longer I weep
If I should die before I wake
Into your kingdom me please take.

Chapter One

I hope nobody will ever have to look at anybody they love through the eyes of an evil spirit. As a hoary-haired woman in the winter years of life, I look back on my journey from a young wife to a widow laughing and crying at the same time. Have you ever literally laughed and cried at the same time? I don't mean have you ever laughed until you cried. I mean laughed AND cried at the same time. I laugh because I feel peace and joy that passes all understanding, I feel as if I am living that scripture. I have never been happier in my life.

My childhood was full of struggles. I watched my parents argue ferociously; I watched my mother struggle to feed us with no help from my father. I watched my father bring my brother a shining new bike for my little sister's birthday. I listened to my aunt and uncle, who lived with us, say vile and horrendous things to one another in anger. I am free from the evil that spewed from my own husband's mouth as he recited Isaiah 3:16-26. He knew it word for word, he emphasized every punctuation in his tone. The scowl on his face and his body language were as the countenance of an evil spirit as he said to me, "Because the daughters of Zion are haughty..." The words no longer ring in my ear. I can't hear it anymore, it wasn't me in the first place, and it never will be me.

I used to think my husband hated me, but looking back, I realize I was fighting an evil spirit in him that he himself did not know how to fight. I look back and find peace. Our heavenly Father knows best, so I hope the good my husband did for others in his life will outweigh the evil he caused us, his wife and children. I forgive him completely for his hatred against me and my children.

I know fully the meaning of Yeshuah's prayer as he hung on the cross, "Father forgive them for they know not what they do." I'm not as good as my Messiah, so I could never fully understand this type of forgiveness. But with understanding, I can easily forgive. I have peace in my new home, my last home. My spirit is quieted, I only hear my thoughts and the worship songs ringing from Spotify on my Smartphone. I feel relief from the sadness of being a rejected wife.

I still cry though, because I feel sad my sons have never had a loving father to guide them and teach them how to be men. They struggle learning to be kind and loving men because they didn't see that in their father. He could not be their example. He was an example of how NOT to treat your wife and children. My daughter has never had a father to be her first love, to show her how a man is supposed to love her. She has never been a daddy's girl. Every girl should know how that feels. I also cry because I have never experienced being loved by a man. My husband could not render unto the wife due benevolence, the evil spirit within him would not allow him to do it. He was the monster under our beds who *terrorized us more than he loved us through his actions.*

What used to confuse me is how he could show so much compassion to other women whose husbands abused them emotionally. I could never understand how the people at the church where we served spoke of him with such honor and respect and so much love. As I watched him perform in the house of prayer, I marveled at what I thought was hypocrisy. When in fact, my husband was actually a good man, a strong man with an acumen for The Word of God like few other men. He was a man deserving respect. At home though, this was rarely the man we experienced. As I think about it, I realize he was literally fighting an evil spirit for his life.

In each moment, as I think about these facts, a single drop of water falls from the tear ducts of each eye. This is good progress because in my youth, I wailed at the thoughts of being a wife rejected. I feared. I felt ashamed and confounded. I felt as if I was forced to live in shame. As a young wife, I never thought I could ever forget the shame of my youth. I was not a widow then, but I still felt the reproach of widowhood, because I lived as if I walked on eggshells every day of my life. I wanted to crave his touch, his voice, his kiss, and his presence, but he didn't offer much of that. He wasn't a touchy-feely kind of guy, unless it was time to copulate; his goal was to show his manliness and skill; all I wanted to do was make love. So, I always felt starved.

My youth was stolen by this evil spirit I did not know existed. I laid in bed with the enemy that was within him for twenty-one years of my life. Still, I could not understand the enemy and how to fight IT, until I found the strength and resources within myself to remove me and my children from its midst. I learned a lot about spiritual warfare over the years, so I know everything I did back then was wrong.

I wasn't born Simchah. It is a Hebrew name, it means Joy; rejoice at heart; spiritual joy. That is the name I chose for myself. Tobiah, my husband, decided my name should be Tamar. It is biblical, from the book of Genesis, she was the wife of Er, Judah's first-born son, and he liked her story. Though I preferred Simchah, he called me Tamar throughout most of our marriage. I was born Paula, named after my father Paul. Paula, no special meaning, no eloquent significance, no expressive interpretation, just Paula.

I am Simchah, a virtuous and praying woman, a cunning, wailing woman of prayer, busy taking care of the needs of my family. I am teaching my daughter to fight spiritual warfare with praise. I am teaching my daughter and her daughter how to pray.

Chapter Two

Simchah smiled after re-reading her final paragraph. She slowly closed the journal and lovingly caressed the cover before easing the leather-bound book into the small chest on the table in front of her. *Drip. Drip.* A single tear fell from each of her eyes as she thought about all the years of blood, sweat and tears that went into filling the pages of those seven journals. Though she knew the battle was never hers to begin with, because the battle belongs to the Lord, she felt a since of victory and completion. Simchah felt like she had finally made it to the finish line. She knew the race was given to those who endured until the end. Her thoughts were interrupted by the sweet sounds of her granddaughter's voice.

"Softah" shouted Zaharah. *"Sister Joanna is calling you. Should I answer your phone? Do you want me to bring it to you?"*

"No, I'll call her back when I finish sewing the bodice onto my dress. I'm planning on wearing it to Chag Shavuot, and I really want to finish this today," Simchah

shouted back.

As Zaharah came into the sewing room, she laid the phone on the cutting table near the sewing machine so Simchah could reach it.

"It gives me great pleasure to dress up for The Lord for the feast of weeks. Plus, the dress I wore for the last feast day is too tight, so I have a good excuse to make myself something new for this feast."

"You know she's going to blow up your phone until you answer, right?" reminded Zaharah. *"She wants you to sit with Saba while she hits the streets with her good time girls!"*

"What do you know about a good time girl?" questioned Softah.

"I hear about Sister Joanna at Bible class when I'm home from school," admitted Zaharah. *"I don't understand how you could keep helping her* anyway. *Saba is not your responsibility any longer. He left you over 20 years ago and he don't even know you anymore. Why haven't you married again anyway? He did and it didn't take him long either."*

"First of all, Saba didn't leave me. I removed myself because I was fed up with being accused! I was tired of weeping and thinking of myself as a victim. I made a choice for your Emah and your uncles; my daughter and sons. I chose to separate from Saba. Second, the scripture says I will be his wife until one of us dies.

Even though he has another wife and even though he has been battling Alzheimer's for the past eight years, Saba is not dead yet. Third, I know you will be twenty-one in a few months, but you need to stay out of grown folks' business. You will never be grown enough to disrespect me or your Saba!"

"I'm sorry Softah. I did not mean to be disrespectful."

"And furthermore, what are you doing to please Yah? Does your good outweigh your bad? You need to be working on that dear heart."

"Yeah, yeah, that's what you always say," retorted Zaharah, as Simchah frowned with displeasure.

"And whether you want to accept her or not, Sister Joanna is his wife, so she's also your Softah. What you need to be doing is watching that young man you're courting to make sure he's a good choice. I overheard your sweet nothings last night when you talked to him on the phone. You know the mistakes I made; don't you make the same ones. Now let me finish my dress in peace."

"Ok? Wait...What! Were you eavesdropping on me last night?" Zaharah protested with a pout. *"Softah, I may never be the woman you are. I don't think I can ever be prepared for that kind of womanhood. She will always be sister Joanna to me, she'll never be Softah. That's a title I reserve only for you, just for the record,"* she confided with a smile.

"Oh, and when can I interview you for my final project on domestic violence. My paper is due two weeks after spring break, and you are my last interview. I want to submit it early so I can wrap my mind around my senior year. I'm going back to campus in 3 days. Before I ask questions, I want to give you time to just tell your story."

Simchah sighed and nodded at her granddaughter. She picked up the small wood and leather treasure chest and pulled out one of the leather-bound books. It was worn around the corners and edges, and the pages were darkened from many years and many tears. Simchah handed the book and then the small chest filled with the other six journals to Zaharah and smiled.

"Zaharah, I have been living my story every single day of my life for decades. The words on these pages amount to more than just a project or a paper. These words give voice to my struggle and give praise to The Most High Yah who delivered me. Just read with an open mind and an open heart. I am sure you will find my story and a whole lot more than you bargained for on the tear-stained pages of this book. We can talk again, after you finish reading."

Chapter Three

I spent many years being embarrassed to tell others my Bible teaching husband was a cruel, emotional abuser. I never told anyone the children ran to their rooms when they heard their father's key in the door each evening, because they feared his moodiness and never knew which mood he might be in when he came home. My children and I were happiest when my husband wasn't home, and no one minded his lateness at all. We actually preferred it. I think it was so easy for him to be cruel because he really believed my only function in his life was in the kitchen and bedroom. He actually said that to my mother years ago.

"I only need her for the bedroom and kitchen," Drip. Drip.

Those were my husband's exact words to my mother. I was humiliated, but not enough to leave him alone, because I had already given my body to him to wife and I feared the wrath of God. My mother cried and feared for my happiness.

My mother warned me: "He'll throw you away like a dirty dish rag".

Those were her exact words, but being the stupid young woman I was, I told her she had no need to fear because he was a man of God, he used the Bible to guide his life so he was bound to change his mind and learn to treat me with benevolence. Man, was I wrong! It never changed. Tobiah never learned to treat me with the love and kindness. The only time he was gentle with me was during sex. As a matter of fact, he rarely touched me unless he wanted sex. Drip.

I wanted to walk away but feared I couldn't take care of the children alone; and I was afraid the sky would fall on me, because The Most High hates putting away. I was afraid I'd spent so much time living in fear and in emotional turmoil at the mouth of my husband that my aged smile, wrinkled eyes, and saggy flesh would be the cause of no other man ever wanting me to wife. I feared being alone more than I feared the cruelty of his scorpion tongue when he walked in the door each evening. Tobiah also told me he couldn't be a father to our baby boy Nehemiah if I ever left him. What kind of crazy thought was that? What do you mean you can't be a father to our son if I leave you? I didn't think he was serious. I thought it was just another control tactic.

Two things gave me the courage to conquer my fears. First, the experience of my oldest son weeping on his high school graduation night gave me the courage to leave. His father accused him of lying and called him a lying dog as he railed on him and slashed his flesh with his scorpion tongue. My boy began throwing his belongings into a garbage bag so he could leave, with no place to go. He was going to run to a friend's home to stay with him and his parents. As I comforted him and begged him not to leave, I promised if he would allow me to help him get to his first year of college, when he came home for the first break, he'd come to a new home. I promised him I would leave his father to be in a safer place and I apologized for having him in such an environment for so long.

Chapter Four

*T*here was no evidence of the scorpion's tongue on our first dates; there were no red flags to alert me. Tobiah wooed me. He was gentlemanly and kind. He opened doors for me, and only gentleness came from his tongue. Abusive marriages rarely start with abuse. In fact, our first dates were probably pretty similar to those of most loving couples. Tobiah was charming, he paid attention to me, and he flattered me. His intelligence and his gentleness attracted me. I was just a babe, naive and wanting. I wanted what every young girl wanted, to live a fairy tale. I prayed for a man who knew the truth so I could follow him into the kingdom of God. I wanted a husband who could teach and lead me. One day, after Shabbat, Tobiah declared The Most High told him I was his wife, I was sent from Him. I believed he was the answer to my prayers.*

Our marriage was not conventional. The minister at the Knesset we attended in those days was a zealot. He needed to control his followers. He told Tobiah it was time for us to get baptized, then married. Tobiah told me, and I submitted. I wanted to be a submissive and dutiful woman of God. We were baptized one

MICHELLE RHNEA YISRAEL

week, and for the first ten years of our relationship we were married according to Hebrew law. Our family and friends were not invited.

We did not have a legal marriage license, so it was our vow we said to one another on a random Sabbath after Bible class which kept him with a woman who he was sure was a whore. The vow kept me tied to a man who had no trust in me at all, one who admitted he didn't need me for anything except to cook his food and satisfy him in bed yet accused me of being disloyal and whorish over and

over again. It was his devaluing of me as a woman of God which made it easy for him to use his scorpion tongue to lash out at me so often. Drip.

At the end of the day, on the way to announce the marriage to my family, Tobiah revealed, "The Most High told me marrying you was a mistake."

He was not reluctant about his revelation. I didn't see that coming at all since he said the Father told him I was to be his wife. Drip. Drip. The next day, I was his lady, I was his dream, I was his wife, whom he SAID he loved, but there was no apology for crushing my feelings.

Chapter Five

*T*he accusation of adultery and the spirit of jealousy actually started very early in our relationship. In the beginning, I was stupid enough to think it was love. I thought it was flattering. The first time was when he accused me of looking at another young man in the church with wanton eyes. I comforted him with loving eyes, I grasped his hand gently and kissed him to reassure him that my eyes were 'wanton' only for him. But it only convinced him for the moment. There was always another time. It never stopped. Drip. I was accused of sleeping with the neighbor and his son, the mail cashier, the gentlemen who owned the dance studio where I took exercise classes, the bus driver, the UPS man or the mailman. Drip.

Once I invited a friend from college, whom I had introduced to The Word, to spend the weekend for the Feast of Tabernacles. I made sure it was okay with my husband first, of course. He said yes and seemed to like the idea of me having a sister friend. As I prepared a space to make her comfortable, I noticed he watched me. While I entertained her during her visit, I noticed he watched me. When she left from what I thought was a really fun and festive feast weekend, he asked me a very *strange question.*

"Have you ever thought of having sex with a woman?" Drip.

I stared at him hesitantly, because I had no idea where this line of questioning was going. I chose to keep my response simple.

"No", *I proclaimed firmly.*

"Why do you ask?"

"Because you seemed to go all out to make your girl-

friend comfortable," *he spat in an accusatory tone.*

I did not appreciate the accusation and I chose not to

respond.

Then he asked, "Who molested you as a child? Was it

one of your uncles or your father?"

I just walked away, into the back of the house to clean up after the festive feast weekend. Later, as we laid down for the night he declared, "We need to pray this spirit of illicit sex out of you. It is an evil spirit and we can be rid of it through fasting and prayer." *Drip. Drip.*

I looked at the ceiling when I responded, because I couldn't lock eyes with him at that moment:

"I will not pray a lie. I will not pray for a spirit of illicit *sex to be prayed out of me that does not exist. It is a lie, so no. Absolutely no, I will not pray that prayer with you."*

Then, I rolled over to face the wall feeling disgusted. I silently wept until I fell sleep. I felt embarrassed and unclean. I allowed myself to be isolated from the companionship of my friend, to avoid such a vile accusation. Drip. Drip. Later that day, I was his wife, whom he SAID he loved, but there was no apology for accusing the men in my family of such atrocities.

Chapter Six

M *e: "Can women have male friends?"*

Him: "No stupid." Drip.

Me: "You don't believe men and women can have a platonic friendship? Have you ever had a female friend? Do you have one now?"

Him: "Whores want friendship with a man who penetrated them before so that when her husband disappoints her, she can be with him, and she doesn't feel like a complete whore, since he'd already been there."

Me: "I hadn't thought of it like that before."

Him: "Hadn't you?"

Me: "You can neither read nor change my thoughts. I was just trying to start a decent conversation."

Him: "How can I have a decent conversation with an indecent woman."

His voice was quiet, calm and calculated. His tone almost made me forget it was just another accusation. Drip.

Chapter Seven

I should have known better but Tobiah's sister's husband, David. called to ask if he could bring their three children to our house because the lights were out in their neighborhood from a storm. He said ComEd reported it would be late in the evening before the power was restored. The children were 8, 5 and 2. David's wife, Marsha and Tobiah were both at work because it was early in the day. As a servant of God, I knew my role was to serve others and I honestly saw this as an opportunity to serve, so I said yes.

When they arrived, I set them up in the living room where the TV and VCR were, so they could be comfortable. I remained in the back of the house with no contact outside of bringing in popcorn and beverages occasionally. My own two-year old played with his children in the front of the house. I stuck my head in from time to time to check to make sure he was being a good boy. The two 2-year olds fell asleep on the floor after they enjoyed the lunch, I prepared for everyone. So, I went into the living room again to put both of them in one of the bedrooms where they could be more comfortable as they napped. Tobiah, stormed into the back door about 3 pm, looked at me angrily, as I sat in the little sewing-area I made for myself in the room off the kitchen. He walked to the front of the house in a rage.

"Nigger get out of my house! Don't ever come to my house again," he yelled at his brother-in-law. "I'm not stupid, nigga. You got a lot of nerve sleeping with my wife and stepping your feet in my house," he screamed as he squinted his eyes in a jealous rage.

All I heard my brother-in-law say was, "Tobiah! Man. What?"

"You heard me nigga!" my husband retorted sternly.

Drip. I was stunned. I was in shock as this innocent man gathered his children and their things quickly. I was utterly humiliated. Then, my husband walked to the back of the house where I stood in shock unable to move. My eyes locked eyes with his as I waited for him to attack me.

"Don't you ever bring your nigga in my house again. You have come to an all-time low, bringing one of your niggas in my house with my son!"

Then, he stormed out the back door to the garage where he did side work as an auto mechanic. Tobiah swooped out as fast as he came in. And me, I didn't know what to say, so I chose to say nothing. Drip. Drip.

"The scriptures say if an unbelieving spouse walked away for a better life and has no desire to return, then let them go. I would welcome a bill of divorcement at this point."

I wanted him to make it fit. He believed I was a whorish wife, which had to mean I was an unbeliever right?

"Then, I would welcome a bill of divorcement at this point, since I am blatantly disrespectful and just plain nasty." I spoke softly to myself.

At bedtime, I was his wife again and we had sex throughout the night as he whispered in my ear, "You have this stiff cock ready for you anytime you want it. You never have to get it anywhere else." Drip. Drip. Drip.

Chapter Eight

I was cooking dinner and he came quietly in the back door from his auto shop in the garage. This time he grabbed my hand and led me to the bedroom. He laid me on the bed and began to raise my dress and remove my panties. I thought he just wanted a "quickie", so I responded favorably so as not to deny my husband. But he didn't want sex, he checked my vagina for semen, to see if I'd had sex while he worked. The problem was he believed it.

"Who was here today?", Tobiah asked in an accusatory tone. Drip.

"Only Odeliyah from Bible class. She brought by a few dresses she wanted me to alter for her. See?", I pointed to the dresses on my sewing table.

"Who else was here?" he interrogated. "Nobody," in

a defensive tone.

"Which one of your niggas did you have in my house?", he countered.

According to Tobiah, he dug for semen in my va-

gina and found it. At least that is what he told the minister when he brought me before the tiny church with charges of adultery. They discussed the woman in Numbers who was given poison. They discussed how to "handle" my whoredom. The ritual of jealousy in Numbers 5:11-31 is a law that both intrigued me and disturbed me. The bad thing is that as they discussed this whorish wife, I considered buying into it. I considered cooperating and having my moment where I would once and for all be vindicated and cleared of these horrendous charges. This law perplexed me as well. I had read it many times. It was the Word of God and I did believe it wholeheartedly, but can I trust these two men? Are they true men of God, does He listen to them? Will He clear me of this charge? Was I regarding the law or these two men as if it were some bizarre and ridiculous process lying somewhere between faith, stupidity or being humiliated?

I knew this was it, I knew he'd give me a bill of divorcement for sure this time. If he truly believed it, then why would he want to stay married to a whorish woman? Why wouldn't he put me away? I wasn't sure how I felt about it. I got up and walked home weeping. Drip. Drip.

Chapter Nine

*T*he emotional abuse I experienced takes time to build. It was slow, methodical and incessant, much like a dripping kitchen faucet. In the beginning was like a little drip I didn't notice. It mirrored an off- hand remark that was, "just a joke." He told me I was too sensitive, and his remark was no big deal. It seemed so small and insignificant at the time.

"I am probably a little too sensitive," I repeated to myself. Drip.

I enjoyed my time alone in the house with my son watching him play and doing my duty as a wife. I read while he napped and kept my tiny garden as he ran in the yard. I thought about how I could learn to negotiate my own life in secret since I was married to a man who would not enable his wife to do great things besides make babies and cook his food. I did not sign up to be imprisoned and treated like a disdained wife.

Black people have been so busy fighting white supremacy that we did not see sexual terrorism in our own homes and communities. We've seemed to use every weapon in our arsenal to protect ourselves against racism and have not held abusive husbands ac-

countable. My grandfather, who fled the south in The Great Migration, experienced the civil rights movement in all its' glory with the marching, bitten by dogs, water hoses, sit- ins, lynchings, and Jim Crow. He would have never believed his granddaughter would fear her husband and his evil rages and the misogynistic imbalanced system of marriage, because he treated my grandmother with benevolence. He didn't look at her submission to him as a weakness or an opportunity to put his foot on her neck, so she'd fear him.

"Am I in a righteous marriage or was my grandmother?" I often screamed in my head.

My grandmother was happy when my grandfather walked in the door after a hard day's work. She missed him. Her greatest peace was when he came home. The fact that my peace came while I was alone, while Tobiah was away from the house, should have been my clue.

I was going in and out of the basement on a really hot summer day in Chicago, to retrieve the laundry from the washer and hang it on the line in the yard to dry. While waiting for the last spin to stop, I noticed a telephone cord running along the top of the wall and going into a piece of the wall I now realized was a door. In the year we lived in the house I did not know there was another room in the basement. There was no doorknob and the door looked just like the wall, it blended right into it.

I managed to open the door and saw the phone cord was attached to another telephone and the telephone was attached to a cassette recorder. I noticed a cassette in the recorder and pushed play. To my astonishment, I heard a telephone call I had with my mother the previous night. I realized my husband tapped our phone. He was recording my conversations.

I saw other tapes with dates six months back and labels in a small box on the other side of the phone:

"w/her mother" …

"w/her sister" …

"w/Leah" …

"w/Brenda" …

"w/Odeliyah" …"

"w/me" (dated)…

There were 3 "w/me" with dates on them tapes.

"So, was he listening back at the conversations he

and I have over the phone and analyzing them?", I asked myself.

"Hmmmmm, why? This cannot be normal, do all husbands do this? Do all wives feel this way?", I asked myself through my tears. There were no tapes labeled Tobiah w/so and so…Why hadn't he heard I had nothing to hide yet? Drip.

If it is unlawful for a man to divorce his wife for any reason then because I am a mere woman, I did not think I stood a chance by pleading my cause to The Most High.

Afterall, Tobiah had never put a hand on me, but his scorpion tongue was all over my soul stinging salacious words all over me. Drip. Drip.

Tobiah was really great at finding Bible quotes to back up his belief that God regarded men more highly than women and he didn't mind sharing them with me in front of my family and friends. He didn't mind letting me know he was always right, and I was always wrong. Not only was I wrong, but I was also haughty, walking with my head held high with my seductive eyes, prancing along, jingling my
ankle bracelets, which I liked to wear.

Chapter Ten

When I go grocery shopping, I like to walk down each aisle one by one. Even though I always have a grocery list to ensure I get everything I need most, walking up and down each aisle to see what is available or what is in season is relaxing. As I walked down the aisle of the grocery store, a gentleman I'd never seen before stopped me in the produce section, as I took my time to fill a bag with semi-soft peaches.

"I recognize you," he said.

I looked to see if my husband was in earshot and eyesight. Tobiah was on the other side picking out pears, he loved pears. Drip.

"I have something for you" the stranger said. "I will be right back."

My stomach felt as if there were knots in it. I didn't move for a few minutes. Then I selected two more peaches, put them in the bag, placed the bag in the cart and met my husband at the pears.

"Who was that?" Tobiah asked.

"I don't know, I've never seen him before," I replied.

"What did he say to you?" Tobiah reviled.

"He asked how to select a good peach," I lied.

Then we headed down the rice and pasta isle. I wanted to find brown Jasmine rice and try a new recipe. Tia Curry Rice. Next, the seasoning aisle.

"There you are," said the strange man as he found me again. "I said I have something for you."

He then handed me my driver's license I lost a little over a year ago. I had since got a new one.

"Thank you," I said confusingly as I grabbed my license from his hand and tried to make sure I didn't touch him.

"I found it outside the Walgreens on 75th street. I meant to drop it in the mailbox, but I kept forgetting."

"Thanks again," I said awkwardly.

I didn't want to appear rude, but how this kind stranger viewed me was of no importance at this awkward moment. I wondered how he recognized me in the store from an ID he has had in his car for more than a year. I had many questions which I knew I could not ask because my husband stood there with his hand on the cart watching my interaction with this stranger. The remainder of our time shopping was quiet. I didn't know how to start a conversation about the encounter *because I didn't have any answers and I knew questions were brewing in my husband's head.*

"You said he asked about picking peaches," he knew I lied. I knew I shouldn't have lied. Drip.

"I didn't want to alarm you." I said. I was sorry, I knew I should not let his jealous rages cause me to lie.

"You are a liar. What else have you lied about?", Tobiah snarled.

"So, you left your driver's license in your lover's car huh?", he reviled. Drip. Drip.

I wasn't sure whether it was a question or a declaration.

"You heard him say he found it outside of Walgreens, remember? I had no idea where I lost it, remember?", I reminded him.

"How did he recognize you from your ID?", he asked.

"I have no idea," I responded uncomfortably. "I thought it was strange too, let's talk about it."

"You think I'm the one stupid," argued Tobiah. I did not weep. As he railed me, I reviled back. Drip.

Chapter Eleven

I never wanted to be the kind of woman to run back and forth or in and out of a relationship. I married Tobiah with the intention of being married for a lifetime. No matter what. My daily prayer was for God to strengthen me so I could. Thinking back, I should have been praying for a way out of this madness.

It had been two weeks since Tobiah touched me. He tried hard not to talk to me. I knew something was up, his silence was the result of another jealous episode.

Drip. Drip.

I declined to ask him who the culprit was this time. Tobiah waited for me to ask why he was angry, but I didn't. We'd been here before and I knew the outcome would leave me in tears again. This was the first time I thought of leaving, but the prophet Malachi said God hates putting away. So, I prayed for God to make me stronger, to take the hard times, to endure until things got better. Is that not what a submissive wife is supposed to do for salvation?

Two days later, we were laughing and having a good time as we watched television and just enjoyed each other's company. I loved my husband's humble spirit at these times. This person, whom I loved to be in his *company, was why I would help his wife take care of the aged Tobiah with dementia.*

Chapter Twelve

I packed up my active little boy, who was not yet 2-
years old, in the stroller my sisters bought for
him, and walked the sixteen blocks to my mother's
house several times a week during the summer. I was
not wired to be alone and I spent too many days alone.
There were people at my mother's house. My siblings
were teenagers and young adults, my aunt and uncle
lived there. Other family and friends came in and out
all day almost every day. It was a happy house. There
was always food cooking, music playing in one room,
the noise of the television in another, and my son loved
playing in the yard.

As soon as Tobiah left in the morning for whatever
it was he left home to do, I packed up to leave for the day.
As long as I made it back before dark, it would be okay.
Tobiah used the daylight time well. It didn't get dark in
Chicago until almost 9 pm and he was usually out until
a little after 10 pm every day. I am not certain what he
did. I had no intention of attempting to find out. I loved
the peace and quiet. Wasn't a wife supposed to miss her
husband while he was away? Wasn't she supposed to be
happy when he came in the door every evening?

The walk did me well, Nehemiah loved it too. He was
intrigued by the cars speeding by and seemed to be de-
lighted by the sounds of the outside. We passed a small

playground in the park on the way. No way could I walk past the swings and slide without giving him a chance to wet his whistle. He did not need to stay long, just a bit. A few slides down the sliding board and at least ten minutes on the swing was enough. He would allow me to put him back in the stroller to finish our journey. It was the day I decided not to stop that he objected with his crying.

"Hey pretty lady," I recognized the male voice and I was angry with myself because I felt a pleasing flutter in my stomach.

"PL", shouted Zack.

The flutter turned to fear of Tobiah following me. He had followed me before. Drip. I saw him hiding be-hind the cars, the trees, and on the steps of some of the houses behind me as I walked. Drip. Drip. I never stopped to acknowledge his presence, I felt he needed to follow me to feel at ease. So, I just kept walking as if I didn't see him. Drip.

"Paula, it's me, Zack."

This time I seemed to turn involuntarily. I quickly locked eyes with him and I couldn't stop the big smile quickly growing on my face and the warm feelings flooding my stomach.

"Zack!" I proclaimed softly, as I checked my big smile in case Tobiah was watching me from behind a tree. "How you doing? It's been a while."

"Pretty lady. You are still a beautiful princess. I thought that was you," he said with a smile. "It's good bumping into you. That smile of yours is still gorgeous."

"Flattery might get you everywhere," the words just slid off my tongue. Zack was always so easy to talk to. That is what me and Tobiah didn't have. We didn't just talk, we weren't friends.

"Hey Sunshine!"

"I'm on my way to my mom's house. I'm stopping in the park though, pull into the parking lot," I pointed south, "it's right up the street on the next block."

Instead Zack parked on the street, got out of his car, and walked with us.

"Who's this big guy?", he asked, while reaching out his hand to Nehemiah. "Hey Lil Man. I'm uncle Zack. How ya doin?"

"This is Nehemiah, he just turned two this month," I interjected.

We began to talk as if the last time we spoke was two years ago. Zack wanted to explore the world and sow his oats as they say. But I found God, I discovered who the negro was, I discovered my heritage and I wanted to explore that. God had my ear, I easily gave my ear to Tobiah, and Zack had no ear for it at all. Zack had enlisted in the Air Force a few months after graduation and headed out to California. Once he left, we simply lost contact. Nobody had cell phones or social media back then so losing contact with family and friends was pretty easy. We did not spend much time together that summer because I was driven to Bible class and Zack was driven to have fun.

Nehemiah had fun that day, he got to stay in the park a lot longer than usual. Zack and I took turns pushing Nehemiah on the swing and catching him on the slide. He even helped him make shapes in the sand. Nehemiah, Zack, and I were happy for a few hours as we played together like children. We sat on the park bench where I could easily keep my eye on Nehemiah playing. Neither one of us looked at each other. Both of us kept our eyes on Nehemiah.

"Man in the Mirror" by Michael Jackson played on the radio owned by the young boy on a bike.

"This song is about a man who attempts to make himself a better man before trying to change the world," I started.

"...yeah, he advises the listener to reconsider his or her life and commit to taking the necessary actions to change."

"...he sees the starving children and he realizes how he never paid attention before," I offered.

"...I don't think he COULD pay attention to it before he took a good look at his own deficiencies and faults."

"...he thought of himself because he could never see the

suffering of others."

"...he could see the homeless man and the woman pretending she is not lonesome...Mike's reference to children not having enough food in their belly's is a juxtaposition of his own wealth. He's making reference to the differences in the poor and people who are well off," Zack noticed.

"...his questions about him being blind can be both a metaphor for a person who is actually physically blind or him posing a rhetorical question because we know people see what they want to see."

"...and I also think he's relaying situations in his life that have really affected him," added Zack.

"...it sounds as if he is giving sound advice."

"...he realized he was being selfish not to consider the needs of others while he lived well...can you see the imagery in, 'a summer's disregard, a broken bottle top,'" asked Zack?

"...yeah, I see a man's inner soul, a carefree summer, loneliness, and depression."

"...a broken heart and his reference to dreams deferred, images of physical scars, hurt and abuse follows the pattern of the wind."

"...he's acknowledging that he is now able to see that there are people around him living and existing with broken hearts," I confessed.

"...and reminds the listener that we have to stop it ourselves, we have to make changes within ourselves. This is when things around us will change," he hinted.

It wasn't a debate or an argument. It was a simple discussion, not complicated. We simply added to one another's thoughts and finished one another's sentences. But I had a real conversation with somebody who cared what I thought, with someone who knew that I COULD think, with someone who cared to hear what I thought.

"Would you rather slide down a rainbow or jump from cloud to cloud?", he started.

"Would you rather have wings but can't fly or gills and can't swim?", I continued with a chuckle.

"Would you rather have a pet dinosaur or a pet dragon?", Zack answered back with a "gotcha".

"Would you rather only be able to whisper or have a very loud voice?", I added with a giggle.

"Would you rather meet a superhero or a cartoon character?", he laughed with his chest puffed out.

"Would you rather live under the ocean or on mars?", I laughed back.

"Would you rather drink sour milk or eat rotten eggs?", he gave a joyous whoop and fist pump!

"Ugh! You won, that's nasty." We both laughed really

hard.

I enjoyed that laugh. I missed talking to my friend. I missed having intelligent conversations with any friend, since I allowed Tobiah to isolate me from all my friends. He tried to isolate me from my family too, but they wouldn't stop coming around or calling and I wouldn't stop walking to my family's home in the warm months. He suggested I only needed him, family and friends were not important. I agreed, but in this connotation, it seemed kind of unusual and even sick.

"I love Michael Jackson's Bad album. Do you have it at home? It seems like you love it too," said Zack.

"No, I'm not allowed to listen to worldly music at home," I replied.

"Hmmmm okay," is all Zack responded. His response wasn't judgmental. We stumbled into a conversation about happiness.

"Are you happy?", I asked.

"I try. What is happening inside us is what makes us happy. We can't allow what is happening around us to make us happy, we cannot allow life's challenges to determine our happiness," said Zack.

"Yeah, you're right. We cannot depend on others to make us happy," I replied.

"Happiness comes from within, from what is going on inside us between our ears, the things we think about,

and the person we are," Zack added.

"The things we allow God to grow in us, this is where happiness comes from," I laughed.

Tobiah rarely just talked to me like I am a human, like I am a woman or a friend. Drip. His conversations were always preachy. He was always trying to teach me and make me a righteous person. When that was not his job. I am the only one who can make me righteous. He claims my salvation is not personal.

"It's my job as husband to teach you," Tobiah always said. Drip.

"But my salvation is personal," I thought. If I have to go before the throne of judgement, I will have to account for my own actions, for the things I did. Tobiah cannot save me. He needs to figure out how to save himself and be more confident so he can stop judging me and accusing me. Having a simple conversation and being treated like a human being felt good. Drip.

"Who is Lil Man's daddy?"

"His name is Tobiah, a brother I met at Bible class. Nehemiah looks just like his daddy's daddy..."

"Is, what's his name again?" "Tobiah," acknowledging his question.

"Is, To-bi-ah," Zack repeated slowly. Is Tobiah kind to

you?"

"Why do you ask?" "I sense something."

"What do you sense?", I was flattered my old friend was concerned.

"I sense that you have lost your sunshine," he revealed.

Silence. Silence. More silence. Drip.

"What time you got?" I asked

"It's a little after two."

"After lunch? Nehemiah missed his lunch. I'm surprised he's not fussy. He missed his nap too. I need to be on my way."

I rushed to get Nehemiah snug in his stroller. Tobiah has probably been blowing up mama's phone looking for me. I try too hard to try to keep him temperate and now how do I explain where I've been all morning? Drip.

"Let me take you Lil Man the rest of the way," offered Zack.

"No, I want to finish my walk," I lied. I did want the ride, but I could not chance Tobiah seeing me get out of Zack's car. I guessed he may be there waiting for me since he couldn't reach me on mom's phone. He was constantly checking on me.

Suddenly I felt like his prisoner. A stupid prisoner. Drip.

"No, I want to finish my walk," I repeated. "It will give Nehemiah a chance to get in a nap before my family is all over him."

I reached in the diaper bag for Nehemiah's snack bag, then gave Zack a big hug. He hugged me tightly and kissed me gently on the cheek. I forgot to look around to watch for Tobiah. I was always watching, but for these few hours I forgot.

"I will be at the house on Winchester for my six- week leave then they stationing me overseas. You can reach me there. Here is the number."

He handed me a small piece of paper I knew I wouldn't keep. I slipped it into the diaper bag, temporarily until I could commit it to memory.

"Don't let him steal your sunshine PL, you don't owe anyone," he advised.

"It was good seeing you Zack, I better go now, my mother has the same phone number and address. Leave me a message there," I responded. "I like our friendship; I love how it feels."

Zack simply responded with a smile.

"Be strong and find what feels right. You found religion and it seems you found a different kind of culture," he added as his eyes admired my garment.

It was the first time in our brief encounter Zack acted as if he recognized my new look. It was a dress I made for myself, lilac and cream cotton with splashes of pastel pink in a kente type pattern, sheer cream short sleeves and thin fringes made into the fabric resemble a Native American style, but with a slim chord of blue, with a thin belt around my waist. Tobiah said he liked the dress because he thought the belt looked like a chastity belt.

A chastity belt? I should have known then Tobiah had an archaic mindset. He would have fit in comfortably with the King Henry VIII, the king who killed his wives at his whim. If he could, he would have me in a chastity belt, used as an anti-temptation device during the Crusades. It would be just the thing he thought he needed to keep me from giving myself to any man who crossed my path. It would be perfect to dissuade me from all the sexual partners and sexual temptations he thought I couldn't keep myself from.

Since Tobiah put himself in charge of my salvation, instead of on his own, it seemed only usual that he would think an unusual thought like the belt on my comfortable summer dress was a tortuous, annoying, and primitive chastity belt, which had nothing to do with The God of Israel and the culture He described in His Word. The chastity belt was created by old evil European men to cause anguish to and control women who could so very easily control themselves merely because they wanted to do the right thing.

The dress had a very thin cord of blue with a match-

ing headwrap and matching earrings. I grew up watching my mother and her sisters put fringes on curtains they hung on our windows. I refused to be lazy and use those same types of fringes on my clothes. I would not humiliate myself looking like my mother's drapes. While I was at home alone so often, I taught myself how to make earrings using cardboard, wire, and fabric.

"I love the wrap too," Zack said, attempting to hold on longer.

I smiled again. I walked away first, headed to my family's home, where I felt safe and secure.

Chapter Thirteen

"*I* treat you better than any other man would,"
explained Tobiah.

I believed it at first, but after studying
couples who appeared happy and watching sisters who
smiled
all the time, I refused to believe that anymore. What was
wrong with me? Why couldn't I be loved? Why couldn't
I be treated with due benevolence? The brothers claimed
that meant all the sex one wanted, but no, it meant
simple human kindness. It was as if I was walking on
eggshells. I wondered when the fear began. I noticed
the drip a few weeks before our "marriage", but I didn't
want to make a big deal of it. I made light of it. I dis-
counted my feelings.

"What is so interesting about your spouse?"

It was the question on the table as we talked with two
other young couples sitting at our table. Each couple
took their turn responding to the conversation question. I listened to the compliments and the exhortations
the couples gave to one another. They were heartwarm-
ing and brought tears to my eyes.

Tobiah, "I don't know the meaning of the word inter-esting." Drip.

Then, he laughed as he pulled me in for a side hug. Drip.

"I was just joking sweetie pie," he laughed. Drip. Drip.

"I have a joke," announced Tobiah. "A married couple is lying in bed together sleeping when the phone rings. It is 2 am. The husband answers the phone and, after a second or two replies, 'How am I supposed to know? We're 40 blocks off the lakefront!' and hangs up. The wife rolls over and asks, 'Sweetheart, who was that?' 'I don't know,' said the husband. 'It was some unsuspecting bastard asking if the coast is clear.' Isn't that hilarious?"

Drip and Drip.

If I said something about the abuse disguised as a joke in front of other people, Tobiah would likely either give me a hug and say he didn't mean it or look at me like I'm crazy because of my reaction. This happened quite a bit in our years together. Drip. My premise is that Tobiah needed to make sure other people believed I was overly emotional so his stories and lies about me stuck. Not long after, Tobiah began to call me stupid.

The feast of Tabernacles 1980 was the first time Tobiah made an insulting joke about me in public. It was common for him to make insulting jokes or put me down when we were alone. He ridiculed my abilities, my personality, my heritage, my family, my education, my cooking, my sewing, my housekeeping. It grew to *everything I did or created or said. But it wasn't all the time. The ridicule came in spurts. If I told him I was hurt, he told me I was too sensitive. The drip was getting annoying, but you don't sell your house over a leaky faucet, right? When a playful joke was a little more than playful, I told myself he didn't really mean it. Drip.*

By the time we got home, the accuser left, and my loving husband was home with me alone. I longed for those moments when he was gentle and kind and loving and complementary. He catered to me that night and made love to me gently. I was drawn in again.

Chapter Fourteen

He used to call me sunshine
said I brightened up his day
said I gladdened his moment
that's what he used to say

He used to smile when I walked up
said I brightened up his day
said I made him feel at ease
that's what he used to say

His friendship never gated me said
I brightened up his day
said I was a special thing
that's what he used to say

*T*obiah took a second job that summer, he was never afraid of work. He worked first shift, so he wasn't off until 3 in the afternoon. On the days I walked to my family's home, he picked me up by 3:30. Tobiah wasn't as astute as he thought; he never even suspected. Zack and I met at the park several times before he was deployed. Our visits were always in public; between brunch until mid- afternoon, with Nehemiah present. We watched him play.

I had so much fun during these simple visits. I made

lunch for us some afternoons. Other times he brought lunch for all three of us. Zack was my friend. I loved our impromptu visits, our mere conversations; our clean, crimeless, inculpable chats. We read "Kindred" by Octavia Butler together that summer. It was a novel which incorporates time travel and intermingles science fiction with a familial slave narrative. It made for engaging conversation, as we talked about our favorite characters. It drew us into conversations about race, marriage, survival, and the dark history of America.

Zack and I never touched outside of a hello or goodbye hug. He never tried to kiss me; he was always respectable, and I made sure I stayed my physical distance. I don't know what Zack was thinking, but I never had any impure thoughts about being physical. I had to prove to myself that I was not a whore and I had no desire to throw myself on any man. It was good having a friend to talk to and listen; someone to treat me with kindness with whom I could just be myself.

Zack told me about a young lady named Faith he met in San Diego that he didn't want to fall in love with. He talked to her on the phone a lot while he was in Chicago. He wished she was his best friend. I encouraged him that it would be as easy to be her best friend as it was to be mine, all he had to do was allow himself to love. My visits with Zack made me feel good about myself. He gave me courage and I encouraged him to open his heart to love. It was a good summer. When I said goodbye to Zack at that first week in, he had no idea I had made up my mind to leave Tobiah and go back to my family home.

My mother knew what I was dealing with when I left home to be with Tobiah after our so-called wedding, with neither his family nor mine to witness and celebrate. She tried to warn me.

"My dear sweet girl, this man will throw you away like a dirty dish rag when he is done with you."

"No, he won't mama, Tobiah is not like that; he is a man of God," I defended him.

"What kind of man of God will take a beautiful and intelligent young woman away from her family and pretend to be married," she asked through her tears.

"Mama, we don't need the White man's piece of paper to prove our love for one another. We said vows to The Most High and God takes it very seriously. We have a marriage covenant we respect," I said quietly.

"Don't do this," mama pleaded. "It's a mistake."

"Mama, you gotta let me go and be my own woman," I said stupidly.

That was the conversation my mother and I had in the beginning, when she should have smacked the taste out of my mouth. Now, I have a son to consider. Tobiah already told me he could not be Nehemiah's father if I left him. I didn't believe him, I thought it was just another ploy to be in control and to keep me from leaving. In the past, if Tobiah suspected I was at wits end and ready to leave, he laid on the charm. He would do things like bring me flowers or candy. He would surprise me with a night out, just the two of us. Once he even whisked me away on a romantic stay at a downtown hotel since we didn't have a honeymoon. During those times he'd be sweet and kind, and I'd fall in love all over again, forgetting about my thoughts of leaving. He modified his behavior just long enough for me to believe he had truly changed.

However, this time, I missed my summer rendezvous with Zack. It wasn't that I missed Zack, I just missed having someone to talk to. I missed feeling valued and I missed feeling I was important with something important to say. I missed that Zack was not there to listen to me, nobody could ball and chain Zack. Tobiah's charm was temporary and I was tired of feeling like I was swinging on a yo-yo. I realized my value and I was tired of allowing Tobiah to fill in the blank spaces with his contradictory constructs.

So, one night, I told my mother I was not going back. Yet, I feared Tobiah enough to leave him with no information and no reasons why. I did not want to get back on that emotional yo-yo and ride until I was strong enough. As if she had been waiting for this revelation, she immediately called my uncle in Michigan City and told him to drive up in the morning to pick me up. He didn't hesitate since he drove from Michigan City to Chicago almost every weekend. My mother knew I needed to hide myself if I was to stay away long enough to wean myself of Tobiah's charm.

I spent the fall season that year in Michigan City with Uncle and Auntie hiding, so I could think and draw close to God for myself. Tobiah was my head, my covering, but in covering me, his covering sprued venom through my soul; a venom for which I had no antidote. I wrote him several letters with no return address and sent pictures of Nehemiah for him to enjoy his growth. I talked to Nehemiah about his Abah and had a picture of him next to Nehemiah's bed so he wouldn't forget his face.

While there I made sure I read my Bible. I read it more that fall in Michigan City than I had at home with Tobiah. I seemed drawn to it now whereas, at home I was drawn to walk those eggshells carefully trying to prevent outbursts and rages. My focus was on the red writing in the New Testament, I wanted to know what the Messiah said about things. I also read about the lives of women and how they related to and were guided by their husbands. Abraham listened to Sarah. Isaac listened to Rebbeccah. And though Jacob had no love for Leah, he did not abuse her. Her torment was caused by her jealousy for the love he had for her sister. I wondered what would happen if Leah would have refused to take her sister's husband. I doubt if her father would have killed her, what else could he have done? Would it have been worse than the torment of being unloved? I knew what being a rejected wife felt like, what could be worse?

I read the story of Samuel's mother, her husband listened to her and comforted her. Boaz was concerned about rumors that would surface if someone in the community saw Ruth leaving his presence early in the morning. He did not start the rumors, he dispelled them. Even Queen Esther was able to get the king's ear to save her people. The men in the community listened to Huldah tell them what the scriptures they found meant and how to respond to what they read. Neither her husband nor the men in the community talked down to her, they listened to what she had to say. Deborah even led Israel in battle, and Barak would not go unless she did because he knew she was the one anointed by The Father. Her husband Lapidoth did nothing to stop her.

There were women in the scriptures who were treated with respect. Moses allowed a bill of divorcement because hard hearted Israelite men mistreated their wives. The Messiah said that too. I discovered Ephesians 5 where it said, "Submitting yourselves one to another in the fear of God, THEN "wives, submit yourselves unto your own husbands, as unto the Lord." I had no problem submitting to my husband. I wanted him to be the head, I was not trying to wear the pants in the family, but when was he going to submit to me? All I wanted Tobiah to do was trust me, love me and stop accusing me of giving myself to other men. I needed someone who practiced the fruit of the spirit and encouraged me to grow in them. Tobiah had it twisted, and I needed to learn to love him from a distance. Placing myself on the outside looking in, I could see more clearly.

I stayed there the rest of August and all of September. Uncle got me a part time job at a tutoring agency, the owner was a retired educator and attended his church. I had four steady clients, a few blocks away. He had been a teacher in the Michigan City school system for 40 years and the agency was his retirement project. It was only open Monday through Thursday from 3:30 - 7:00 pm. He had twelve school aged children and six high *school students who were still struggling in basic skills. I found out at the agency that I had a natural ability to teach. I planned to go to college to become an educator. He had two other tutors, besides me. One was his nephew, Wayne Banks.*

It seemed Wayne was a local celebrity. He sang in my family's church choir on Sunday, or should I say he blew the place up with his voice. I attended church on a few Sundays with Uncle and Auntie every now and then. Their church had a really energetic praise and worship team. It's too bad the Israelites I know couldn't get with it. I never understood why because the Bible study seems to be for us, but the praise and worship is in accordance to the Word of God. I read in the book of Psalms, "Praise ye the Lord. Sing unto the Lord a new song, and his praise in the congregation of saints. Let Israel rejoice in him that made him: let the children of Zion be joyful in their King. Let them praise his name in the dance: let them sing praises unto him with the timbrel and harp." This was enough for me to know we should be praising God as passionately as we teach His Word.

Sometimes life puts you on a path and won't let you off. Wayne taught me that our paths are controlled by our choices. The energy we put into making these choices is what puts us on these paths. So, then, it is not life who puts us on a path, it's me, you, he and she. We do it to ourselves. Wayne was a path I should not have chosen.

He sang at the local bar several nights a week. He was good at drawing people in. His charm and charisma made people want to listen to him and follow him. And to top it off he was fine. He was a good looking, Black man with beautiful dark chocolate skin as smooth as butter; standing tall, about 6 feet 3 inches and more self-confident than Sidney Poitier. Wayne was, in fact, too self-confident; he was arrogant and cocky. He was a sexual predator and it was common knowledge his history was to groom young women he deemed vulnerable and train them to be his secret sex pets, but nobody told me. It's a good thing he wasn't a minister. He'd misled tons of folks and had no remorse about it. And his bull's-eye was me.

I think Wayne was skilled in giving girls mad butterflies. He put a huge smile on my face when he looked at me. It was crazy how much I liked him. The old women would say, "he made my head swim." I forgot about right and wrong. I forgot about my strong desire to be a wife and be loved, instead of looked upon with disdain. I forgot to keep my panties pulled up and my dress pulled down. Some nights I'd fall asleep talking to him on the phone and wake up a few hours later and he'd still be on the phone. I wished I had a marriage license so I could tell him I was married.

Wayne took me to the club to listen to him sing on a Friday night. I knew the Shabbat was beginning, but my plan was to simply listen and not buy anything. I was fooling myself. After the set I went to his dressing room, so I wouldn't feel like I was in the club on the sabbath. He had another set to go and I thought I'd wait it out in there. He was easy to talk to, as easy as Zack. He didn't mind me talking to other guys while he was in the room.

We didn't look at it as a threat, he seemed to trust me. He'd simply come over and hold my hand or put his arm around my shoulders. He moved with a crew of other young cocky guys and their girls. He wasn't intimidated by my intelligence and liked it when I dressed up; Tobiah preferred I dress down.

Wayne never missed it when I did my hair differently, he always noticed and loved it. He was not overly protective. Wayne was much more charming than Tobiah, full of compliments. He called me "Pretty Lady" each time he greeted me. It felt good. After the final set that Friday night, the time I knew I should be at home reading Bible stories to Nehemiah, Wayne insisted I go with him to an after set at one of his guy's houses. I went with no resistance.

Twenty minutes into our arrival, Wayne was on the other side of the room giving all his attention to another young lady. Then, her young man was on the couch sitting a little too close to me making small talk. The host of the house brought out joints in a small bowl and pills on a small platter, for what he called, "everyone's enjoyment". I noticed Wayne rejected the bowl of joints and opted for the platter of pills instead. He then pulled out a small white plastic bag half full of a white powder from his jacket pocket. He made two small rows of the powder on the table in front of the love seat where he and the other girl sat, and they had at it before they began to kiss. My mouth hung wide open.

I looked over at the guy sitting next to me, he had told me his name, but I didn't really hear it. When I looked at him to see if he saw his girlfriend and my boyfriend

kissing, he asked me did I prefer a joint, pills, or what Wayne had. Then, he leaned in and tried to kiss me. The host and a girl, who was not his girlfriend, were busy in the large chair on
the other side of the room and another couple made their way to the bedroom.

I felt as if there was a spirit in my left ear saying, "Go ahead, don't be a prude, kiss him; a pill will get you there faster than a joint". In my right ear, I heard "Therefore to him that knoweth to do good, and doeth it not, to him it is sin". I got up and left. I walked as far as I could and stopped at the gas station to call Uncle to pick me up. He asked questions on the way to his house that I avoided.

When Wayne called later that night I didn't answer. I didn't answer when he called the next day or the day after that either. I ignored him at the tutoring agency on Monday. Tobiah was not good for me, but as I thought of Wayne, I knew I could not fix a disaster by creating a catastrophe. I wasn't sure if I had committed adultery or fornication and there are not levels to sin in God's mind. What is it called when boyfriends swap girlfriends? I know when couples are married, it's called wife swapping. It was too much for me to comprehend. Call me old fashioned but I like a man who would not trade me with his friend at his whim. I was not going to be turned into a harlot nor a drug addict! No way!

"Father forgive me for being weak for companionship," I prayed deeply that night. "I'm sorry, Father, against you only have I sinned. Please accept my sincere repent-

ance. I will try to do better and be better." I pleaded. "I got myself in this mess and I need you to help get me out of it."

I'm Sorry

*I am so sorry, Lord Adam, please forgive me for getting
us into this mess
I should'da listened to you, I should'da walked away
when I heard it wasn't your voice
I should'da told you when that serpent first spoke to me
How can I ever be trusted again?
I am so sorry please forgive me Lord.*

*I promise to help you all I can
I promise to do my part while you work to till the
ground by the sweat of thy face*

*I promise you Adam, you are not alone
I'm here to help you till these thorns and thistles
The herbs of this field are not as pleasant as those we
ate in the garden.*

*But I promise I will do everything
I can to make them pleasant to your taste and pleasing
to your palate
This tent our new home is not as pretty as the garden
and
It doesn't smell as good
But I promise I will do everything I know how to make
you comfortable in it.*

I'm here Adam, I promise to help you all I can
The Lord said my desire would be to you, my husband
He said my sorrow and my conception would be greatly
  multiplied
He said I would bring forth your children in sorrow and
  great pain
I will try to be a good mother to your seed and our
  children
I will try to help you teach them in the way they should
  go.

You are to rule me my husband
I hope you can find it in your heart to have mercy on me
I hope you can rule me with kindness because of what
  I have done.

You are my head, my desire is to you my lord
Oh my God..., These curses are too deep for me
I can hardly bare it Lord what will happen to us? What
will happen to our children?
Oh Yahuah, Jesus, Jehovah, Yahweh, God I'm sorry
I should'da listened to Adam's instruction.
Please forgive me.

    I was thinking of enrolling the Community College,
but it would be too difficult in Michigan City. I didn't
have a car, the buses didn't run as well as in Chicago,
and my mother and sisters were my support system. I
needed help with Nehemiah if I was going back to school.
I had to find direction for my life if I was going to be
single again and raise my son. I also did not want to keep

Nehemiah away from his father too long. A boy needs his father. I had been away long enough to be strong enough to know that I did not have to be Tobiah's wife any longer, but he would always be
Nehemiah's father and he needed to know where Nehemiah was so he could pick him up for visits. Since we had no lawful marriage license, this was an easy out of an uneasy situation.

I felt free to make decisions and draw close to God on my own. I also needed to get back to Chicago as my family prepared for the holidays. They made a big thing out of Halloween, Thanksgiving, Christmas, and New Year's and I didn't want Nehemiah around it. They had small children and they wanted their children to have a good time during this season. I didn't want to confuse him, and I didn't want to offend my uncle and his family because they had been very good to me us while we were there.

Nehemiah would be safer in Chicago because my mother was not that into the holidays. Her celebrations took place at her church, she didn't decorate or anything so Nehemiah couldn't learn to admire the festivities. My sisters were young women living the life of a young woman of the world, but they didn't care much about decorations and
holiday parties, they just wanted to be pretty and fly, be cool, and be amazing to their other young friends. But they loved Nehemiah, and didn't mind babysitting at least sometimes, all I needed was their sometimes.

I needed to get away from Wayne, he was not good for me either. So, I decided to leave my uncle's hospitality a week before Halloween, when the decorations would be put up. I arranged for my father to drive to Michigan City, since he lived in Benton Harbor, and drive me back to Chicago. He asked me why I didn't come to Benton Harbor, and I appreciated the offer, but I knew I would have the same problems there since he was a musician and he was on the road a lot.

I wouldn't have a support system to take classes in somebody's college and I would need a car. CTA and Metra were plentiful and easy in Chicago. Nehemiah would be three soon and I needed to figure out what to do with my life. My sisters could rotate caring for him while I was in class. And Chicago State University was only 5 blocks away, I could walk.

I seemed like a good plan. I had no thoughts of running into Tobiah; I was past his charm. It was September 23rd and I had a plan. My father would pick me up October 25th. I had one month to work my plan. I sent for the admissions papers to Chicago State so I could be in class in January. The admissions packet arrived in only 3 days and I would have it completed and mailed back the same day. The school would have it back before I arrived.

"Thank you for giving me another chance," he gently whispered in that charming voice that took away my mental and emotional strength. "I promise I will do right by you," he whispered.

"You promise Tobiah?", I countered with more confidence than I had before.

"I took you for granted and I apologize, please forgive me," he appealed.

We were back to the usual pre-Michigan City escapades in less than a month. Before I knew it, I was in the midst of the cycle of abuse again. The honeymoon was over, and I was being accused of sleeping with every man who crossed my path again. It wasn't better after I told Tobiah I was
nine weeks pregnant. It wasn't worse either. It was the same as before. I wrote Wayne a letter telling him about the baby, but he never responded, and I was glad. My admissions application was accepted, but I never stepped foot in a classroom. Over the years I learned Tobiah could control the evil spirit that inhabited him for up to six months. I learned to enjoy his charm and his love three to six months at a time.

Tobiah never mentioned Wayne. He accepted my pregnancy and took care of Wayne's daughter like she was his own. I appreciated him for that, and his attempt to forgive kept me with him for so long.

"I know we don't need man's piece of paper to make us married, we made a covenant with one another, but it didn't quite feel like I was married. Maybe if we had it, I wouldn't have made that awful mistake with Wayne."

I persuaded Tobiah and we got that marriage license, but our families still weren't there. We went to city hall. It was a compromise for a wedding and loving witnesses.

Chapter Fifteen

"*E mah, why you sad all the time? You don't like me? You don't like to watch me play in the park no more,*" *Nehemiah asked inquisitively.*

"*I love you Nehemiah. You are a gift to me from God. I love to watch you play,*" *I comforted my young son.*

I didn't realize I was frowning so much, and I certainly did not want my unhappiness to affect my babies at all. So, from that day forward I plastered a smile on my face. I stood in the mirror and used my fingers to put the corners of my mouth in position to smile. Once I saw the smile, I wanted my babies to see, I closed my eyes to feel the smile. I wanted to be able to show my children that smile without looking in the mirror. My children deserved a smile.

Every morning when I opened my eyes, I didn't want to raise my head from the bed until I felt a smile on my face. I lay there awhile as I listened to Tobiah prepare himself for his workday, hoping the children wouldn't wake from the noise. I laid there with my eyes closed to talk to myself so I could make it through just one more day. Inside my head, I also sang and prayed. Some days

I didn't want to breathe anymore but my children kept me going. They were given to me to nurture and to love. The Most High helped me, He heard my cries and one day I couldn't cry anymore. My tears dried up and before I knew it, I didn't have to plaster a smile on my face anymore. It was through Christ that I found myself strengthened.

Tobiah had names ready for the boys, but he didn't have one ready for Salachyah. I didn't hold it against him. I understood. I was not in a position to push. I wondered if I had another girl if he would want to name her. My baby girl was no mistake. She brought so much joy to my heart. The Most High sent her to me as he sent King David his son Solomon after his chastisement. Salachyah would grow to do great things too because I was going to nurture her with prayer and love.

Chapter Sixteen

*T*he man who dropped off the diapers for diaper service. The man sitting at the light waiting for it to change. The brother who volunteered to teach martial arts to the boys at the church. The brother hired to teach math at the school where I worked. The stranger walking past me in the store. The owner of the stance studio where I took Zumba.
The brother who cut the neighbor's grass. The cashier at the grocery store. Or any other man with whom I accidently made eye contact. The accusations were continuous. It was always unexpected, and it was still utterly ridiculous and extremely hurtful.

If I cried or acted like my feelings were hurt, I knew I needed to be ready for the ridicule like it was my fault he hurt me with his tongue. As if I caused it because I was too sensitive anyway. According to Tobiah, I didn't have anything to be upset about.

"You aren't even good for a good fight," I heard often as I tucked myself in the corner chair to cry.

There were many days I allowed the demon to steal my joy. My sunshine was very sparing. Like a yo-yo, his temperament would be the exact opposite. He was gentle, used kind words, and even looked at me as if I *was beautiful in his eyes. He spoke of my goodness and what a peaceful spirit I had. Sometimes he loved me, and I knew it and felt it; and other times he had a disdain for me I found too difficult to bear. I was riding a roller coaster. Yet, I loved the good in him. I began journaling to help me deal with my feelings. The constant drip of that damn faucet was not going to damage my children.*

Why I Write

I write because I
hear what the voice of many waters' sings
get weary of turbulence in this life
praise Jesus the Holy King
cry because I am hurt
love to laugh instead of weep
am thankful he brought me from the dirt
wait in haste but desire to trust
pursue patience, virtue and knowledge
am being trained to shy from carnal lust
need my maker to purge sin he sees
want to be healed of the old wound and scar
thirst to deliberately stir emotion in others
love to teach young minds and shake them ajar

I write because I
feel music swirling deep in my bones
can hear the praise song in my head ring
am quickened by the rhythm in the sound
help proclaim the nobility of my people
propagate, enlighten, diversify, and expound
am part of a glorious people's past
feel the hurt and harm piercing from the bondage
want this knowledge to help our future last
pray for tender mercy, loving kindness, and the seal
love to praise and pray to The Most High
need to solidify my own inner beauty and zeal
need to reaffirm my inner strength with speed

desire to dwell in the house of God
aspire to always trust His lead
want to thank Him for allowing me to see
need to increase my faith in my Lord
seek a greater joy than man has given me

I write because I
hear the music and the song in my pen
suddenly have a whole lot to say
consistently fall and make crazy mistakes
want to leave a legacy for my precious young
understand that salvation sits on high stakes
am aware of spiritual wickedness in high places
study the cause of powers and principalities
love to put smiles on stressed out faces
have a story to tell
have a mission to reach
needed to come out of pity's shell

I write because I
flutter as I feel the cadence beat
feel a joyous pulsating trance
love the sound to jump me out of my seat
find understanding, strength, and power in my pen
seek to comfort my sentimental spirit
need a love that seems far beyond men
have done everything I can think of to do
won't give up but don't dare fall
hold on to what I know is true
lift His name on high everyday
am glad I know Jesus and the plan
am grateful for all blessings and the narrow way

Railing and Reviling

Reviling is to scold as scold is to taunt

Taunt is to chide as chide is to criticize.

Criticize is to rail as rail is to find fault with.

Find fault with is to beat down as beat down is to terrorize.
Terrorize is to judge as judge is to intimidate.
Intimidate is as a slap in the face
A slap in the face is as malign.

Unrighteous as thieves and liars.

Sinful as adultery and drunkenness.

Wicked as idolatry and the effeminate.
Intolerable as Sabbath breaking and the slothful.
Unjust as extortion and those who covet.
Hated as the talebearer and discord sewn.
Despised as innocent blood shed.

Intimidate is to despise as despise is to hate.

Hate is to castigate as castigate is to curse.

Curse is to threaten as threaten is to unkind language.
Unkind language is to condemnation as condemnation is to attack.
Attack is to mistreat as mistreat is to berate.
Berate is to abuse as abuse is to accuse.
Accuse is to murder as murder is to crime.

Seeds of pride and envy.
Fruit of wrath and strife.
Purposed from envious and pernicious.
Meant to defame and beat down.
Implications of judgement and imprudence.
Not in accordance with right and justice.
Kiss New Jerusalem goodbye.

Chapter Seventeen

*A*s I stood on the choir stand, just before the music started, I spotted Zack coming in the door with his wife, Faith, and their children. She was obviously the one for him and at first glance, they looked pleased with one another. Last I heard she caused him to settle down and stop sewing his royal oats. I was happy for him. He sent pictures of his new babies after each birth. I waited a long time to see him walk through that door and join me on the road to salvation. This was a surprise. I couldn't wait to meet his wife and give her a big hug. I was happy to praise God that day.

"Like Jesus, I wanna please him; walk in his ways, commandments keep them"

Mark, the brother leading the song, was not a likeable brother. I rarely said much to him other than, "Shalom brother Mark, how are you and your family?" He rarely admonished anyone, especially sisters. His communication wasn't pleasant, until he combined it with his larynx and his diaphragm to blow the heck out of a gospel song on the Sabbath. I preferred songs that worshiped and praised Yah, and this song was more of a "teaching" song than a "praising" song, but it was most definitely one with a good melody that could make me move my feet, hands, head, shoulders and arms. And that is just what I did that day.

I closed my eyes, rolled my shoulders, bobbed my head, and grooved to the soft flow of music that permeated my whole soul that day. The choir director made a clapping motion directing us to clap, but it wasn't a clapping kind of song. It was a snap your fingers kind of melody and that is what I did. I knew my part well, so I closed my eyes for moments in the song. My feet joined in perfect sync to the beating of the heartbeat of the song. My good friends standing on either side of me in the alto section were used to my dancing on the choir stand and they moved away slightly to give me the space I needed to enjoy myself. We had an unspoken agreement.

As the song progressed, I felt relaxed, and allowed a small smile to form on my lips. My knees and shoulders moved in sync as I sang the words in prayer asking Yah to help me be like His son, whom he sent to this earth to die for my sins. It was a perfect and moving moment of praise and gratitude. Wasn't it okay to dance and sing praises to our God? Wasn't it alright to really connect with him in song and think about how much I wanted to be like Him? Wasn't it fine to praise Him because His name is excellent?

I did not want it to end, I wanted to extend it; we could have sung that song twice. I hadn't had enough. That song was da bomb and that day it was better than ever!

The brothers who wrote and arranged this song moved the hell out of me. Not only the melody and arrangement moved me that day, but I was moved by the lyrics too. I loved singing in the choir. I sang alto and the alto part the choir director gave us was fire! It was my favorite part of Sabbath service. The Bible class was enlightening, and it was definitely necessary, but studying was for us. The time provided the choir to praise and worship was for The Father. It was our time to praise Him.

I made a big mistake on the choir stand that day. I should not have enjoyed the music so much. I should have thought about Tobiah and his reaction to my praise and worship, instead of focusing on The Most High God. I forgot about Tobiah. When I climbed off the choir stand and sat next to Tobiah and the children, when our eyes locked and I gave him a warm smile, he met me with a hellish stare.

"So that's your new nigga?", Tobiah snarled in his hellish mood.

I broke out in a cold sweat, paralyzed and humiliated, because the sister and her husband directly in front of us heard what he said. They looked at each other in confusion, then quickly turned their heads to the front of the church, frozen trying not to move. I knew Tobiah did not mind making a scene, so nothing came out of my mouth. I
felt stuck, surprised, hurt and helpless.

Turned out there was a rumor going around the church that Brother Mark was having an affair with another sister in the church. The grapevine discussed it after class, sisters were convinced it was a single sister whom Mark was attempting to add to his family. Abigail said her husband thought it was just a rumor. He did not like to add to vicious rumors. However, Tobiah had other ideas.

Before leaving, I moved through the crowd to find Zack and Faith. When I got to them, I hugged Faith first so as not to get off on the wrong foot.

"Peace and love my sister," I giggled. "I am so happy to finally meet you. My name is Paula, people around here call me Simchah."

"I am happy to meet you too, Zack told me a lot about you," Faith shrieked.

I loved her warm and lively response. I liked her a lot. I gave his children a big smile as I hugged them and introduced myself. She was happy. I knew Zack had it in him to make someone happy.

"Hey Sunshine!", he remembered.

"Zack! What are you doing here? I saw you coming in from the choir stand."

"I saw you up there jamming. You were really into that song. I was hoping we could talk before we left," interjected Zack. "We started attending the class in Houston Texas a few years ago."

"That's so exciting Zack," I am so happy for you and your family. You have got to tell me how that happened!"

"We are in Chicago for a few weeks for my father's funeral,' he responded.

"Oh, I am so sorry for your loss, when are the services?", I sighed.

"We actually had it Tuesday. We will be here for two more weeks. We need to pack up the house, I am deciding whether to put it on the market or rent it," Zack informed me. "How's the little fellow, Nehemiah? What's he up to?", he wondered.

"Nehemiah is a young man. He's away at college," I answered. "I have, wait for it, five sons and my daughter is 15. Her name is Salachyah, it means forgiveness. She brings so much joy to my life. She has the tenacious spirit I lacked most of my life. I hope to spend time with you both before you leave," I said in earnest.

Turning to look at Faith, "Do you need anything while you're here? Call me and I will help you pack up the house. Maybe we can even get a few more sisters to come help. I know moving is hell. I hate it. Let me give you my number. Please feel free to call me. I know of a really nice spa in the South Loop and we can have lunch or something. It's not easy being a stranger to Chicago."

"Would you rather slide down a rainbow or jump from cloud to cloud?", I looked at Zack and said.

"Would you rather have wings but can't fly or gills and can't swim?" he continued with a chuckle.

"Would you rather only be able to whisper or have a very loud voice? Faith added with a giggle. We all cracked up.

"You know the game?", I asked Faith as we gave each other a high five.

It was a nice moment. The look on Zack and Faith's faces said thank you. They seemed relieved.

"Come, let me introduce you two to my husband, To-biah," I beckoned to them to come to the back where To-biah and I were sitting. But he was not there. I couldn't find him anywhere. The boys and their bags were also gone. I was embarrassed.

"We need to get out of here anyway Sunshine," Zack relieved me of the awkward moment. Faith and I gave each other another big hug and I made her promise she'd call me to come help her pack up Zack's father's things.

I had choir rehearsal and a feast committee meeting, so I did not leave right away. By the time I got home and found Salachyah with the boys, I knew I was in the center of an episode. The children were happy to see me and asked why I didn't come home with them. Tobiah left them home alone. We heard Tobiah's keys in the door a few hours later. As was the children's custom, they ran to their rooms when they heard the key scared of the mood their father would be in when he came home. They could sense his mood was not pleasant and opted to remain in their rooms to play.

I fed the children, put them to bed, and I decided to

ask Tobiah what he meant by his statement to me in church. I knew what he meant but, I was afraid to stand up to him. His will was much stronger than mine and his words pierced deeper than I could think but, I had to ask this time. I just had to know why?

"You know what I meant, you got a new nigga huh?", he repeated.

"I just don't get why you keep accusing me of this heinous act. I want salvation. I want a spot in the kingdom. Why don't you know that by now?", I asked. "Why do you think this is true?" I looked him in his eyes.

To my complete and utter surprise, "I know it's true because God told me it is true," he hissed.

As usual, I abandoned my idea to stand up to Tobiah this time. Instead, I completely shut down, as usual. My heart skipped several beats. My eyes could not make contact with his eyes. My tongue felt as if it had been cut out. I could not find the words to respond because this was just not the usual accusation for which I grew accustomed. He really believed with all his heart he got these messages from Yah, The Most High. I stood there not able to move.

"If it is not true, I give up my right to the tree of life," said Tobiah believing what he said with all his heart and might.

My thoughts didn't know where to go. Who is the accuser? The word accuse means to charge with a fault or *offense. I quickly reflected. I was floored. I was motion-less. My feet were glued to the floor. Why in the freakin frack would a sane person even think to give up his right to the Marriage of The Lamb for a marriage built on torment and not worth the paper it's written on? The one thing I did know is that it was not God whispering in Tobiah's ear. That scared me and caused my bones to quiver under my skin.*

My mind rolled back memories of all the times he accused me. "So, this is why he believed it with his whole heart," I thought. I finally understand why he would storm in the house as if he knew someone else was there. I understand why he followed me hiding be-hind the trees as I walked to my mother's house. This is why he talked to himself behind closed doors as if he were in pain. He doesn't talk to himself. He talks to an evil spirit. This is why the voices behind the closed door frighten me. Because the voices are demonic. I under-stood why he really believed I was having an affair with his sister's husband. "I understand it all", I concluded as I saw these words on the page.

I tried my best to love Tobiah, but he wouldn't let me love him enough. I wanted so much to be obedient to God and be an obedient wife. All love is not good, and all obedience is not holy. It was in each moment as I stood motionless and speechless, that I mustered up enough good sense to make a decision to remove myself and my babies from that house. I should have done it years ago, long before we conceived six children.

Was this the same voice that spoke to him when he was told I am his wife? Then this was not a marriage from the God I read about in the Word. That stupid statement, the one where Tobiah gave up his right to the tree of Life, the Son of The Most High God, Yeshuah Ha Meshiach, Jesus Christ, the Rock of Salvation, The Rose of Sharon, The Kings of Kings, Lord of Lords, now that's stupid! I was afraid not to relinquish his control over me. Who was Tobiah really following while I was following him? The answer to this question gave me the strength to get the hell out of there once and for all.

I had to be prepared for an outpouring of love and affection. I realized a long time ago that my husband was a misogynist and he had the ability to turn on the charm at the drop of a hat. This time, I would not fall for it. Tobiah grew to be a good provider and I loved him when he was Tobiah. It was the demon I needed to leave. When I figured out how to get out, I was out.

Scorpion's fire

scorpion's fire ensnares the soul disobeys
the noble heart
pouring pestilence into the ear language
discord weigh not words
can't give virtue breath jaded monster mocks
beauty poison deceits set with skill
eat of treacherous passion
subdues softly contaminates love subtle
whoredom accused cunning adultery cited

jokes the honest bed love never
tainted suspicions void of wit
convinced affections shared for sport feverish
flame repeatedly spoken throwing restraints
unwarranted criticism treachery from
youth purged true love causes lonely to roost
silhouettes of wicked ears who saw envy
eyes heard strife feelings of
wrath whispers of Satan who is the
accuser an evil jealous spirit
causes one to mistreat abuses your
blessing venomous saga
the secret lie
causes much anger
scorpion's fire pisses God off

Chapter Eighteen

W henever you find yourself in the hands of someone who does not understand your value, purpose and destiny...you will find someone who will use and abuse you. Someone who abuses you, does not understand you. The best thing you can do is remove yourself. Let go and let The Most High deal with that individual. Again, do not allow someone's dysfunction to cause you to sin against God, destroy your peace or give you bad energy.

Finally, after 21 years of living in the fear of emotional turmoil, I mustered up enough strength and courage to remove myself and my children from the grips of the mean man. Tobiah was my cross to bear and I bore it as long as I could. But what happened? My family was happy and helpful. I praise Yah He put in their hearts to help us so much with our transition. They thought I would stop living the lifestyle in which I believed. They thought I'd attend church with them on Sunday, eat the pork I hadn't eaten in years and take part in the holiday celebrations again. When these things didn't happen, they became a bit standoffish with me again. I think they just didn't understand where I was coming from and they didn't get my pain.

Change is painful, and it is very difficult to embark on the unknown. My lifestyle was still unknown to them. But it was not completely their fear of change. I was the oldest child of my eight siblings and when I embraced the Israelite lifestyle, I set my self apart from my family more than I should have. I was the one who stopped communicating. I considered my church family more family than my blood family. I was wrong. Instead, I should have been an example to them.

I could have converted them with love. It's the love we show to one another that will push us into Yah's kingdom. The Scribes and Pharisee kept the law better than anyone, and they won't get in, because they had no love. I pushed my family away, instead of drawing them into the light of Christ. My behavior was not the salt of the world. I didn't pray for them. I didn't act like a loving elder sister for many years, and that pushed them away. I did not involve myself in the intimate parts of their lives, showing them love. I had to try my best to make sure me and my children would not fall by the wayside. I had to make sure I put our lives in the hands of The Most High. Prayer became was my fortress and praise became my weapon.

There is a thing known as domestic abuse. It comes in physical and emotional betrayals. The cycle of domestic abuse must stop. It cannot be stressed enough. Do you think The Most High intended for "and thy desire shall be to thy husband, and he shall rule over thee" to be void of
love and kindness? Don't you think He intended for

men to lead their households applying the Fruit of the Spirit? How long will the contrary messages be taught to our daughters and sons? When will enough be enough? How long will it rent hearts before its end comes?

Let the records show these few statistics for women between the ages of 14 and 44. Domestic violence is the leading cause of injury or death. It kills more than auto accidents, muggings, and cancer deaths combined. 88% of children who live in homes where domestic abuse occurs are violent. Approximately 8,800,000 children in the U.S. are at risk of father abandonment when daddy resents mom's strength to embark on reestablishment. Or at risk of either witnessing or suffering domestic

abuse.

Almost 1/3 of seniors (adults aged 59 and over) in the U.S. report being abused by their children or grandchildren, having been beaten, cursed and often neglected for their money or belongings which they possessed. It effects everyone, regardless of age, race, ethnicity, sex, social, or economic status. It leaves devastation that modifies many young and old of us. The abuser is all about control. It is not and never was or will be about love. They are angry at themselves for feeling inadequate in some way or pain they themselves saw and experienced as they grew up. Their subconscious believes it is the way it is supposed to be. They live in denial but won't admit it; nuts and crazy, blind and can't see.

Oh, we do know when we are abused. We don't want to admit it to neither ourselves, nor especially not to anyone else. We make excuses to cover up the crime, we are ashamed; but all we seek is the love and acceptance from our abuser. Our reason is that we love them. With all their flaws and impaired ways, we truly love us some him. He sees a vulnerability in a woman, and he uses it to manipulate and control. He sweeps the victim off her feet, the fairy tale Prince Charming Dream— like it's a whirlwind romance. He either locks her down in a relationship or marries her quickly, usually within two months often with no familial witnesses, so slickly.

Then, he systematically cuts her off from her support system, either by moving away or by complaining so much with his tongue "they hog your time" or "I don't like them, and they don't like me". His goal is to detach her support and systematically cut it off gradually, until she spends less and less time with her family or his, and especially friends. This time is crucial, since this is the time when the "fun" begins.

He doesn't like the way she dresses. He doesn't like the way she wears her hair. She becomes the object of his flaring tongue. "You are so stupid". "You are too fat." Or conversely "I will love you no matter how big you get." "You are trifling, you are lazy, you are…" Just fill in the blank. Until, there is no more of the real you, remaining on this sinking ship's plank.

Your self-esteem is perfectly destroyed, then may come the physical smacking or not, maybe a more constant and severe tongue lashing Then he says, "I'm sorry, I will never do it again", which is called the "honeymoon period", or phase four if you will. Then, it starts all over again; up and down, off and on, in and out won't be still.

The average domestic abuse victim leaves their abuser seven times before they leave for good—or die— could be a spiritual or physical death. Or wait she may plot to hurt him and are successful to a dismal and deadly despair. How many will be the charm for her? She could be "merely" called every name in the book. Humiliated in public or not spoken to and ignored for six months, feeling his anger at every stare. She could be stabbed, raped, beaten, thrown down the stairs or beat down til she doesn't care.

Still she goes back. No one understands how completely defeated a victim feels if they have never been one. This is the hardest thing for a friend or family member to watch. They put their all into helping the victim get out, to help a loved one successfully leave a bad situation and then they don't leave or then they go back to the source of sheer vexation.

Tobiah never hit me, so I was confused about my own abuse. I talked to women who went back to their abuser after suffering horrible injuries. One woman got hit in the head so often she always had a black eye and is deaf in her right ear. I talked to a young pregnant woman whose boyfriend tied her down, beat her in the arms and legs til they were swollen, not wanting to hurt his unborn child. I know women who have had broken limbs after "falling down the stairs". Where is the honor of man and wife? Others "only" suffer emotional trauma, leaving she and her children debilitated for life.

Deciding to leave or stay and risk being killed by or killing someone instead is a task more difficult than breathing. More children suffer, become unproductive, and are at-risk—being witnesses to abuse, than being at-risk due to poor or husbandless parenting. You don't have just you—to think about, what about the children? What are their chances of being abused or even being the abuser who mars? This situation is as dangerous as children running in front of passing cars.

I see a lot of men asking for a God-fearing woman. Then the Lord sends you one and you, in turn, sends her away. So, The Most High sends you another and you treat her bad. How many more do you think he's going to send you? A King has no intention of trying to change, control, or "shut up" a Queen. A mentally mature man wants his woman just as strong and tactfully outspoken as him, with her own mind, because he knows his woman's strength is a reflection of his own and fully understands that iron sharpens iron. A weak man, on the other hand, only approaches weak minded females, so he can be an Alpha male by default. Only in my pain. did I find my will. Only in my chaos, did I learn to be still. Only in my fear, did I find my might. Only in my darkness, did I see God's light.

These are not made up scenarios and facts, this is an undeviating domestic violence pattern. And if you recognize yourself in these statistics, there is only one thing to say...get out now. And don't go back; slowly and carefully make life new. As I live, I have come to see first-hand, some men are victims of abuse too.

My church 'family' labeled me a whore, a sinful woman, a liar, an unruly female, and a troublemaker. The men feared me because "he" said I committed adultery. The women feared me because they thought I wanted their husbands. They all feared me, because my *silenced spirit made me look as if I were a rebellious and stubborn woman. Rebellion is as the sin of witchcraft, while stubbornness is as idolatry. Nobody wants such a woman around. So, I was shunned.*

I could look someone in the eye and say "Shalom" and they would look at me in disdain and walk away without saying a word or uttering a sound. They refused my contributions for the feasts. Someone tried to push me off the choir stand after we sang and were dismounting. My good friends stopped calling, they stopped looking for me after Sabbath class, and they avoided me instead. If they saw me coming their way, they'd turn and walk in the opposite direction. They acted as if they were afraid of me. They never mistreated my sons, but my daughter was labeled and targeted because I was her mother. The other young girls were not allowed to play with my daughter.

I was crushed in the church I loved. They proved they were not my family. I was afraid I would be alone for the rest of my life, with no loving husband, a family I was distant from, and no real friends. So, I put my focus on making sure my children and I did not abandon God's commandments. I made sure I put my children in situations where they could gain healthy friendships. I enrolled them in baseball, softball, dancing, swimming, and other fun activities. I made sure each Sabbath we got up early and prepared ourselves to keep the day holy. I lived without the fellowship of friends and the closeness of family. I thought about living this life of fear and I realized, I was not afraid of death at all, life seemed to be a whole lot more painful than taking my long rest.

I knew I was not wired to be alone but, being alone was better than being tormented.

I learned to write to release energy and gain strength. Over forty years of experiencing hurt is difficult to encapsulate, so I chronicled my pain on the pages of the journals I kept through the years as I searched for freedom and healing. Through journaling, prayer and praise, I found the power The Most High placed within me to defeat the enemy within. I have the power, because The Most High gave to me. Luke 10:19 says: "Behold, I give unto you power to tread on serpents and scorpions, and over all the power of the enemy: and nothing shall by any means hurt you."

I Got the Power

*I got the power down inside myself to
stand up to your put down.*

*It came from the same spirit that
led old Noah around.*

*Like Noah, I can stand as you toot
your mouth to scorn.*

*I understand the atmosphere that
caused you critic to be born.*

*No more will I run and hide so my
eyes can be filled with tears.*

I've grown stronger in the Lord you see
all these teary tearful years.
You critic can think what you want to think.

For I now know that it's your values and not
mine that causes this awful stink.
You, critic, tried hard to lower my self-esteem. But
not even you can change the Lord's mind when
he chooses me too for his team.

You have the power to alter this distorted
bond. Until then, I will yearn for you to
know but, there's no need to respond.

Consequently, I got the power down inside myself
and I am neither angry nor afraid anymore.

The Lord Jesus in his magnificence
is that firm effectual core.
In him only shall I fear

As the time of the end draws closely near.

Vengeance is not mine of course
Gotten past the heartache with much remorse.
Jesus comforts me when I am filled with sadness
and sorrow.

He's shown me how to use his word for the strength
I need to borrow.

His everlasting arm is bringing about healing
from damages incurred.

In his word there is true restoration wisdom
and counsel preferred.

His word solidifies the foundation for
which loving kindness rest.
Thereby loving him I sincerely do my best.
Moreover, I got the power to be strong enough.
I got the power to be humble enough.
I got the power to be obedient enough.
I got the power to be faithful enough.
I got the power to be peaceful enough.
I got the power to be forgiving enough.
I got the power to be joyous enough.
I got the power to be patient enough.
I got the power to know enough to keep my eyes
on his word, for only therein lies my power.

Chapter Nineteen

Zaharah walked into the room with the last journal in her hands and put out her arms to hug Simchah.

"Wow Softah, I never realized everything you went through in your life", Zaharah sighed as she held Simchah in a tight embrace. *"I stayed up all night reading your journals. I could not put them down. You are such a strong woman. Now I know why. I don't know what makes you stronger, the fact that you stayed with Saba for so long or the fact that you finally left him after so many years. And after everything he put you through, you still have*
enough strength to take care of Saba?"

"My life living with a husband who could not control his demons has taught me that Elohim gives the hardest missions to His most elite soldiers. I am a soldier in this army of The Lord. My time with Tobiah didn't break me, it made me strong. I will love my neighbor as I love myself, because I love Yah and it is the right thing to do, so yes, Zaharah. I will help Joanna take care of your

grandfather because it is the right thing to do." Simchah nodded as she held Zaharah.

"And Saba took care of your mother. He gave her his name. He fed her and provided for her. Though he was not a touchy feely, love 'em up kind of father, he was equally hard on her as he was all the boys, Tobiah never made a difference between his sons and Wayne's daughter. He wasn't perfect, but he had his good."

"Grandma! What are you telling me? Are you telling me that grandpa is not really my Saba?"

Zaharah stared at Simchah in dismay and disappointment. *"Softah? I can't believe you've been acting perfect all my life, like you haven't made mistakes."*

Taking her granddaughter by the hand and looking her in the eyes, *"First of all, Zaharah, I never told you I was perfect. What makes a man or woman righteous and perfect is that when they fall, they get back up and they never make that mistake again. They may make another one, but not that one. Second, you don't get to judge me. I advise you to spend your energy getting the beam out of your own eye. How perfect are you? My last advice to you my dear is to that there is a kind of love that gives you the courage to cause you to want to be a better person and you can have that kind of love. It's the kind of love that makes you feel anything is possible. Hold out for it, you deserve it."* Zaharah nodded and smiled at her Softah's words of wisdom.

"When you fall in love, fall in love with the man who wants to know your favorite color and just how you like your tea. Fall in love with the man who loves the way you laugh and would do absolutely anything to hear it. Hold out for the man who puts his head on your chest just to hear your heartbeat. Fall in love with the man who kisses you in public and is proud to show you off to everybody they know. Wait for the man who thinks you are the most beautiful woman in a room of beautiful women and who only hears your voice among them. You deserve the man who makes you question why you were afraid to fall in love the first place. You want the man who would never ever want to hurt you. You want the man who smiles at your flaws and

thinks you are perfect in every stage of your growth. You want the man who loves to wake up to you every day. Wait and choose wisely so you won't have to learn to endure the hardship and pain from a bad marriage. There is too much other pain we must endure. Right?"

"Kan, Softah."

"Once our choices get us into hot water, we are too quick to run from the discomfort and pain of it all, from relationships that are less than ideal, because of our hastiness. Sometimes The Most High causes us to endure hardship and harshness for a higher, redemptive purpose because we refuse to hear his voice in the first place. Sometimes God's teachings are forged through hardship," Simchah sighed wiping the tears from her eyes. *"Do you hear me Zaharah?"*

"Loud and clear, Softah."

"Realize too that man will not be perfect. He will have his flaws, as do you. The Most High is witness to he and the wife of his youth. You and he will be one, that means you are a part of him, and he is a part of you so identify the beams in your own eyes and pray them out. If you are focused on the beams in your own four eyes, you will not have time to be a busy body trying to get the mote out of the eyes of others." Simchah said lovingly, as Zaharah nodded and smiled.

"And don't idolize your husband so much that you hold him above God causing you not to communicate properly. Don't be afraid to tell him what you like and what you don't, after you talk to God about it of course. And that's it. That's my story and I am sticking to it," Simchah deeply exhaled and smiled.

"Thank you Softah for sharing your story with me, but now can we talk about the part where..." Zaharah pleaded.

"No, I don't feel like there is anything more to tell," Simchah's response was interrupted by her cell phone vibrating.

"I better answer this. Sister Joanna is probably wondering why I did not call her back last night. Let me get ready to be humble and smooth things over," Simchah said putting on her best smile.

"Good Morning Sister Joanna. Peace and love," Sim-

chah sang, *"How are you?"*

Simchah's bright smile suddenly faded and turned into a look of deep concern and sadness.

"Oh, I see...I was in the middle of a project and couldn't answer the phone," she admitted, then quickly inhaled and shook her head as she closed her eyes and listened intently.

Zaharah tried to figure out what was going on, but Simchah put her finger to her lips to tell her granddaughter to be silent while she continued to listen.

"Wow, this is very unexpected. Let me get dressed and we'll be right over," Simchah sat her phone on the table as two tears streamed down her face.

"What's wrong Softah?", Zaharah asked with concern and confusion.

"Your Saba took his long rest Zaharah. He passed away in his sleep last night."

"What? No Softah!" Zaharah cried out.

"It is finished," Simchah exhaled a deep sigh of relief, because she was finally free.